KAY THOMPSON'S

ELOISE'S

WHAT I ABSOLUTELY

DRAWINGS BASED ON THE ART OF

HILARY KNIGHT

_____

What I
Absolutely
Love Love
Love

_____

(the one I absolutely love love love)

LOVE LOVE LOVE

Simon & Schuster Books for Young Readers

NEW YORK · LONDON · TORONTO · SYDNEY

SIMON & SCHUSTER BOOKS FOR YOUNG READERS

An imprint of Simon & Schuster Children's Publishing Division

1230 Avenue of the Americas, New York, New York 10020

Copyright © 2005 by the Estate of Kay Thompson

SIMON & SCHUSTER BOOKS FOR YOUNG READERS

is a trademark of Simon & Schuster, Inc.

"Eloise" and related marks are trademarks of the Estate of Kay Thompson.

Book design by Cheshire Studio

The text for this book is set in ITC Bodoni Seventy-Two.

Manufactured in the United States of America

2 4 6 8 10 9 7 5 3 1

Library of Congress Cataloging-in-Publication Data

Thompson, Kay, 1911-

Kay Thompson's Eloise's what I absolutely love love love /

drawings based on the art of Hilary Knight.

p. cm.

Summary: Eloise lists some of the things she loves including

room service, the ballet, and Eloise herself.

ISBN 0-689-84965-6

[1. Self esteem–Fiction.] I. Title: Eloise's what I absolutely love love love.

II. Knight, Hilary, ill. III. Title.

PZ7.T3716Kax 2005

[E]–dc22

2004013017

ELOISE'S
What I Absolutely
Love Love Love

I am Eloise
I am six
Here's what I absolutely
love love love

The arts
(so uplifting)
I am wild about
the ballet

I enjoy to parler Français
Sometimes here's what
you have to say
"Pardonnez-moi Cherie my dear
but I am a little petite fatiguée"

Ooooooooooo
I absolutely love
my rag doll Sabine,
who has shoe-button eyes
and two right legs and
no face at all

Here's what I like to do
Dress up

even when it's rawther chilly

or when I am a grande artiste

I absolutely depend
on the basics

Ooooooooo I absolutely love
Room Service
They always know it's me
and they say "Yes, Eloise?"
And I always say
"Hello, this is me ELOISE
and would you kindly send
one roast-beef bone,
one raisin and seven spoons
to the top floor and
charge it please
Thank you very much"

Here's what I adore
Nanny
Emily
Weenie and Skipperdee
New York
Paris
Moscow
and The Plaza Hotel

I am also at home
in the country

My needs are few

Food (filet mignon)

Shelter (The Plaza Hotel)

Clothing (Dior)

Oh I am absolutely
content with everything
(as they say in Paree)

But more than anything else
I am rawther fond of . . .

Me

ELOISE

and you're trés fantastique too

OTHER BOOKS
YOU'LL ABSOLUTELY LOVE LOVE LOVE

The Absolutely Essential Eloise

♥

Eloise at Christmastime

♥

Eloise in Paris

♥

Eloise in Moscow

♥

Eloise Takes a Bawth

♥

Eloise's Guide to Life